GOD MADE EVERYTHING IN THE WORLD

This is another story about God making our wonderful world. He made all kinds of interesting and beautiful living things and put them on earth.

GOD LOOKED at His beautiful new green earth, and sparkling rivers and lakes and seas, and God said, "That's good!" This was the fifth day and God said, "I'm going to put something in the waters. I will fill the waters with all kinds of fish." So He did.

THERE ARE little tiny finish, and middle-sized fish, and great big fish. Some fish are bigger than an automobile. God saw all His fish, and thought they were very nice indeed. He liked them so much He said, "Raise families of fish. I want more and more of you."

NEXT GOD made birds of every kind and color. They sang and few about and were very happy with the happiness God shared with them. God looked at the birds He had made and blessed them. "I want more and more of you to fill my world with song. You are so pretty!"

NOW IT was the sixth day, and God had already made many things. But he kept right on working. Next God made all kinds of animals: dogs and horses and cows and pigs and sheep. . . .

AND ELEPHANTS and giraffes and kangaroos. . . . .

AND LIONS and tigers, and pussy-cats, too.

BESIDES all these big animals, God made small jumping ones, too. He made frogs and toads and grasshoppers and butterflies and beetles. And God made crawling and creeping things, that we sometimes think we don't like very much–caterpillars and worms. Crawling and creeping things are very wonderful. We would like them if we knew more about them.

GOD MADE so many kinds of animals, that we could never see their pictures all at once. God looked over all His new animals, and thought they were very nice. "Have families," He said, "be happy in My beautiful world with the warm sunshine and cool rain."

WHY DO YOU think God made this beautiful world, with moonlight and stars, and sunshine and rain, and flowers and trees, and animals and birds and fishes, and grasshoppers and butterflies? God was making a home for you! God loves *you* so much, He thought of you when He made the world! And God made the world for children everywhere. God loves *all* His people and thought of them all when He made the world.

NOW FOLD your hands and close your eyes. God is listening. Whisper, "Thank You, dear God, for making the world. You thought about me and made things for *me*, I want to think about You and do things for You. You love me. I want to love You, dear God. Please teach me how to love You more every day."

THINGS TO MAKE

(Cages for small toy animals)

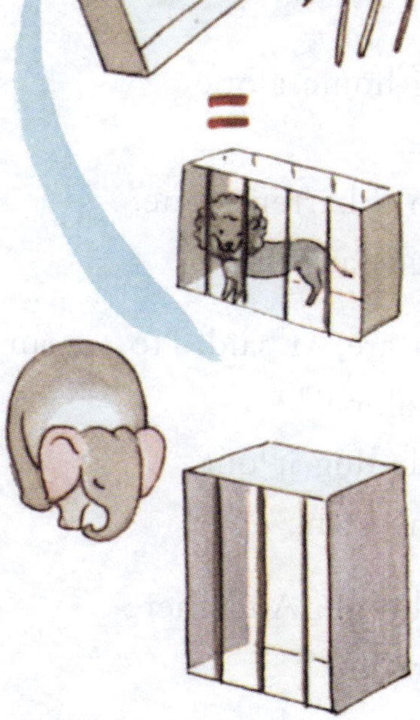

Have you ever thought of playing zoo with your small toy animals? You can make cages very easily out of small boxes and toothpicks or lollipop sticks.

Make a row of holes about 1/2 inch apart with a steel knitting needle along the two long sides of the boxy. Try to make the holes exactly opposite each other so that the bars will push through nice and straight.

Now you can decorate the boxes and put signs on them.

If you want to make circus wagons, you just add wheels by taping two sticks across the bottom of the cage and sticking four cardboard discs on the ends.

My Tree

As I was walking home alone
I saw a little tree,
wedged tightly in a barren stone,
Yet it grew straight and free.

"How proud you are," I said, "to sprout
Here bravely all alone!"
I bent, and gently dug it out
To keep it for my own.

I took it in my house. And there
I gave it ample room.
And yet—for all my tender care
It would not grow or bloom.

It hung its branches as in grief.
I thought I heard it sigh.
Or was it just a falling leaf
As I was passing by?

"What makes you wilt and bend so low?"
I whispered, "Answer me."
Did I not give you room to grow
And nurse you faithfully?

And suddenly I heard my tree
with gentle voice reply:
"More than your care and company
I need the sun and sky.

I need to root in deeper ground
Then all your vessels hold.
My branches need the winds around,
To make them strong and bold.

And storms and rain must weather me
To make me unafraid,
That some day I may shelter thee
Beneath my roof and shade."

Was it the tree, was it my heart
That spoke? How do I know?
But quickly I agreed to part,
That it might live and grow.

I set it on the mountain high,
Where winds blow strong and free.
And sometimes, when I'm passing by,
I rest beneath my tree.

THE RIGHT OR LEFT GAME

For this game you need some toothpicks and a die. Everyone starts off with the same number of toothpicks—at least ten apiece. Then the die is passed around, and each player has to give as many toothpicks to his left neighbor, as the number he throws. Anyone who runs out of toothpicks is out of the game. The last person *with any toothpicks* left is the winner.

You can also play this game the other way around: each player has to give as many toothpicks as the die says to his right neighbor. Then the player who is the first to be left *without any toothpicks* wins.

WUPSY PAYS A VISIT TO THE QUEEN

There are some devils who give more trouble than others. It is not that they are particularly clever, it is just that silly people listen to them.

Wupsy saw one of them one evening crawling around Sunny's hut. It was a long lanky devil, a dirty gray color that made Wupsy think of some nasty disease. He knew he must now allow that sort of devil anywhere near Sunny so he flew down right in front of him. He was not afraid.

The devil came quite close before he noticed Wupsy, then he shivered and crawled away as fast as he could. Wupsy chased him till he disappeared into a hole in the ground. Then he flew back to the tree where he had been sitting.

Most nights Wupsy spent looking at God and the more he looked, the more he could see, and the more he saw the more he loved God and the happier he became. That is why Wupsy was always to happy. He simply couldn't help being happy.

Tonight, though, he was worried and he looked at God even more carefully than usual, in case there was anything God wanted to say to him.

God did tell him something, or rather He showed him something because God does not have to use words. He showed Wupsy the Throne of God in heaven and he saw the Queen of Heaven who seemed to be calling him.

Wupsy knew he must not keep the Queen of Heaven waiting for she is the Queen of Angels too. He darted quickly up to heaven, while the great stars rolled by him. He went first to the Throne of God as every angel does who comes to heaven, then he went straight to the Queen. There were lots of angels there to see her about things, but they knew she had called Wupsy, so they made way for him. He went and sat at her knee and looked up at her to tell her he loved her so very much.

She wanted to know all about Sunny because she was specially interested in the people at Matongu and above all, the babies who had been baptized.

Wupsy told her Sunny was not quite so small now. He explained:

"You see, he eats and eats and gets bigger and bigger every day. All babies do. They are always putting bananas and beans and other things inside them, so they have to get bigger to make more room."

Mary smiled, for she had had a Baby once Who got bigger every day, though He probably did not east as many bananas and beans as Sunny did. She asked if he had much trouble with Sunny.

“Not much *trouble*,” Wupsy answered, “though I *do* have to be careful. He’s always chasing and fighting other little boys, but he doesn’t *mean* anything. They are really playing and no matter how hard they fight, they’re not a bit cross with each other afterwards.”

The Queen nodded wisely. Then Wupsy suddenly said,

“Wouldn’t it be funny if angels wanted to have a fight just for fun now and then. It wouldn’t do at all, would it?”

The Queen smiled at this and she said that when Sunny got bigger he wouldn’t want to fight quite so much, for though small people fight when they are happy, big people only fight when they are very cross, and she hoped Sunny would never get that cross.

“Then of course,” said Wupsy, “he doesn’t always do as he is told, but mostly because he forgets. He can’t keep everything in his head at once, and some things get pushed out. His mother Ntaka-Ntaka doesn’t like it when the things she says get pushed out but you really can’t blame him, can you?”

The Queen looked serious and said,

"Yes, I know, that is why I called you here to come and see me. You know Jesus wants Sunny to be a priest one day. Well, the devil will do his best to spoil everything, so you must be very careful."

Wupsy jumped up and knelt at Mary's feet and said:

"I know, I shall take good care of him. I think it is wonderful that God chose Sunny to be a priest some day. But though I shall be careful, please will you help too? I'm always asking God about it, but He never refuses you anything at all. Everybody knows that!"

The Queen of Heaven smiled again and said she would do all she could, but, she said:

"A good deal depends on Sunny and on you. God never forces people, and Sunny must work hard himself. He will have to fight devils just as hard as he fights the other little boys. If he does his best and you do yours, there will be nothing to worry about. You can be sure I'll help all I can and when Sunny gets bigger, make sure that he asks me himself, too."

Wupsy would have liked to go on talking to the Queen, but there were some other angels waiting to see her, and they were in a hurry. So he said good-bye and went to kneel close to the Throne of God a little while before flying back to Matongu and Sunny.

MAGIC PICTURES

To think up and draw magic pictures is a lot of fun. They are simple to make. Draw the main part of the picture on a not-too-heavy piece of paper. Now add the "magic part" on the other side. When the paper is held against the light, the original drawing shows through. It works best if you place the paper against the window-pane while adding the secret touches. For instance, you could draw a chicken in an empty nest on one side, then draw a few eggs on the other side in the place where the nest shows through. By looking at the picture on the table, right side up, all you will see is the chicken in the nest. But as soon as the picture is placed against the light, the chicken will have laid its eggs!

To make the illusion more complete, you could even paste another thin sheet of paper on the back, after the picture has been finished, to hide the magic make believe. Everyone will want to use his own ideas for a picture. A fisherman with a net, who catches a fish which is drawn on the other side, is a good idea, and a house with bare windows, with all the family with smiling faces looking out, drawn on the other side, can be very funny when held against the light.